I0692295

For my buttons: Noah, Milo, Zen and Lotus

www.theenglishschoolhouse.com

Copyright 2021 © by The English Schoolhouse

All rights reserved. This book or any portion thereof may not
be reproduced or used in any manner whatsoever without
the express written permission of the author except for
the use of brief quotations in a book review. This is a work
of fiction. Names, characters, places, and incidents are a
product of the author's imagination. Any resemblance to
actual persons, events, or locales is entirely coincidental.

ISBN: 978-1-955130-16-5

Phoenix the Flower Kid

By Dr. Tamara Pizzoli ✳ Illustrated by Neneca

For Phoenix Cruz, the best three things in life all started with the same letter: family, food, and fun. Whenever one or more of those three were around, Phoenix was sure to have a ball.

Half of Phoenix's family called them "the machine" given the remarkable amount of food they could put away at lightning speed.

The other half called them "the dishwasher" because they were known to clean their own plate, as well as everyone else's in sight.

If they weren't studying or sleeping, Phoenix could be found outdoors with the neighborhood kids.

Who had the time for television when there were bikes to ride, balls to throw, and friends to catch?

Phoenix's favorite day of the week was Saturday. That's when their entire family would get together at Abuelita Carmen's house from brunch until long after the sun went down.

There were so many tíos, tías, and primos who showed up weekly, sometimes it seemed like they might not all fit. But Abuelita Carmen insisted there was always room for one more.

While Phoenix's mother Ilaria and tías swapped stories and *chisme* while preparing tamales, mole, enchiladas, elote and tostadas for lunch and dinner, some of Phoenix's cousins stayed inside and made up games like "hair salon" and had singing competitions.

Rain, snow, or shine, Phoenix could be spotted out on the lawn or in the street, organizing troops for an imaginary battle, overseeing a fierce game of Red Light, Green Light, or leaving their cousins in the dust as they raced barefoot in the street.

One Saturday evening after a long, hard day of playing, Phoenix's mother stood at the doorway and called all the kids inside for dinner.

Phoenix beat everyone as they raced to the front door, and took their place at the table after washing their hands.

As Phoenix looked around at the large family, it was clear that joy and love were also present in the room.

Phoenix's father dinged the end of his fork slightly against his glass.

"Ok, familia," he began, "today is a special occasion. Natalia has an announcement to make."

The family sat quietly as Phoenix's aunt, Tía Natalia, stood with her boyfriend Manuel close by.

After a short pause, the pair shrieked, "We're getting married!"

The dining room erupted in cheers and applause.

It took no time before Tía Natalia was bombarded with questions.

"Have you picked out your dress?"

"When is the wedding?"

"Who's making the cake?"

"How many people can I invite?"

Phoenix was chomping happily on their chicken tamales when their Tía Tina asked,
"Have you picked the flower girl?"
All of Phoenix's girl cousins gathered closer, their ears perked and ready.

"Yes" Tía Natalia grinned,
"I'd like Phoenix to be the flower girl."

The room fell silent.
Phoenix paused mid-chew, then gulped.

Cousin Maria finally blurted out,
"Phoenix?! But...but...they don't even like flowers!"

Late that night, after most of their aunts, uncles and cousins had gone home, Phoenix caught a bit of their mom and aunt's kitchen chatter over cafecitos and pan dulce. Tía Margarita began, "Dulce or Ana Karina obviously would have been better choices for flower girls, Ilaria. I've never even seen Phoenix in a dress..."

At that moment,
Tía Natalia snuck up behind Phoenix and playfully pinched their arm. "Eavesdropping, eh?" she laughed.

Phoenix looked down before starting,
"Tía Natalia..."
But when Phoenix went to say more,
the words were nowhere to be found.

Exactly two weeks later, practically every woman and girl in Phoenix's family accepted Tía Natalia's invitation to shop for the wedding dress. Phoenix tagged along and sketched in their notebook while everyone else swooned and sighed.

When Tía Natalia found just the right dress, she asked Phoenix for their input.

"I think you look incredible, Tía," Phoenix smiled.

Weeks and months passed.
The day of Tía Natalia's wedding was quickly approaching. Everything was perfectly planned and in place...everything except the flower girl's dress.

On a Tuesday afternoon, Tía Natalia made arrangements to pick Phoenix up from school. Where there's understanding, words often aren't needed.

"I have an idea," Phoenix grinned as Tía Natalia drove to the tailor.

Phoenix was deliberate and decisive, and explained their vision in great detail. They selected the fabric, and the tailor perfected the fit.

The seamstress cut and measured while Phoenix sketched ideas for embroidery.

Soon, the day of the wedding arrived. Phoenix noted that despite all the weeks and months of planning, the moments leading up to the ceremony were pure chaos.

As Phoenix's aunts and mother fussed over every detail of Tía Natalia's makeup, dress, hair, and nails, Phoenix slipped into their tailored outfit, laced up their kicks, and stood in a nearby corner.

As the guests were seated and the music began to play, the wedding coordinator approached Phoenix with a basketful of petals and a genuine smile.

"They're ready for you!" she grinned.
Phoenix nodded and thought a moment.
Then they grabbed as many petals as their fists could hold, and stuffed them into every pocket they had.

And when they were given the green light, Phoenix ran down the aisle, tossing fistfuls of joy and bliss into the air as the audience looked on expectantly.

When Phoenix reached the end of the row, Tía Natalia emerged with a beauty so breathtaking, everyone was left speechless. But before she began her walk on the petals, Phoenix's eyes met their aunt's as Tía Natalia mouthed three words to her niece, "You look incredible."

And once the vows were said and kisses given and dances danced and feasts eaten, everyone had to admit that the bride was truly spectacular, but the flower kid, in all their unique splendor, proved to be a rare and memorable gem that would not soon be forgotten.

Moral of the story:

Be You.

www.ingramcontent.com/pod-product-compliance
Lightning Source LLC
Chambersburg PA
CBHW041546240626
47164CB00003B/146